I Live
in a
Mad House

KAYE UMANSKY
I Live
in a
Mad House

Illustrated by Katie Sheppard

A & C Black • London

For The Odd Job Boys

First published 2007 by
A & C Black Publishers Ltd
38 Soho Square, London, W1D 3HB

www.acblack.com

Text copyright © 2007 Kaye Umansky
Illustrations copyright © 2007 Kate Sheppard

The rights of Kaye Umansky and Kate Sheppard to be
identified as the author and illustrator of this work respectively
have been asserted by them in accordance with the
Copyrights, Designs and Patents Act 1988.

ISBN: 978-0-7136-8416-2

A CIP catalogue for this book is available from the British Library.

This book is produced using paper that is made from wood grown in
managed, sustainable forests. It is natural, renewable and recyclable.
The logging and manufacturing processes conform to the
environmental regulations of the country of origin.

Printed and bound in Great Britain by MPG Books Limited.

Chapter One

It was the half-term holiday and I was out washing cars with Josh Mahoney. We were in business together. It was supposed to be a joint enterprise, although you'd never know it.

I had thought of everything.

I had provided a sponge, for a start. (It was my little brother Kenny's bath sponge, actually, but he has a flannel, too, so I reckoned he wouldn't miss it.)

I had provided old towels for drying, old rags for polishing and a stiff brush for getting dirt off wheels. I had also brought along a bottle of special car-washing shampoo that I'd borrowed from my dad. (I intended to replace it before he found out, with the money I would earn.)

Josh's contribution was a rusty bucket he'd found in a skip. The handle was wonky and it leaked quite badly. He was meant to have brought along some rubber gloves, too, but he'd forgot.

Some partner. I wasn't impressed.

We'd been at it for hours and done four cars in Josh's road. We'd earned eighteen pounds so far, all down to my efforts. I'd done the talking on doorsteps, explaining about our luxury service and telling them how much it would cost. Most people acted like Scrooge, although we only charged four pounds, which was a bargain.

Josh never said a word.

After they'd seen the magnificent job we'd done, a couple of people had kindly given us a fiver. That made up for the ones who slammed the door in our faces. One old lady threatened to set her Pekinese on us. You meet all types, knocking on doors.

It was a warm day and we were finding it pretty tiring, traipsing in and out of strange kitchens and up down strange hallways, slopping water all over the carpets and knocking over bicycles. Some people got quite shirty, although they could see we were having trouble with the wonky bucket.

I was keen to carry on, though, because I was desperate for money. I needed a new skateboard. I'd left my old one out in the garden for five minutes and someone had stolen it. My parents were sympathetic, but not enough to buy me a new one.

I'd spent all my savings on a present for Kenny. His third birthday was coming up, and I'd got him a big plastic water gun and a fireman's helmet from a charity shop. Together, they cost seven pounds fifty, which was very generous of me, but I knew he'd love them.

So I was penniless. I needed a board. It was all down to me to raise the cash.

Mum needed a lot of persuading about the car-washing business.

'There are a lot of funny people out there,' she said.

'Really?' I said. 'I haven't seen any clowns lately.'

'Don't be silly,' she said. 'You know what I mean.'

Then I promised to be sensible and said I was doing it with Josh and we'd only knock on the doors of people we knew. In the end, she reluctantly agreed.

The board I wanted cost a massive forty pounds. I'd seen it in a catalogue. It's similar to the one Josh has got.

We were splitting our earnings down the middle, so altogether we needed to earn eighty. Twenty cars. Ten a day. Say half an hour a car. Two days' work, maybe. Less if people were generous. More if we had trouble finding customers. I had it all worked out. I was taking this seriously.

Josh, however, was flagging. He was sitting on a wall, watching me spread lather over car number five, which was a small, filthy, mud-caked van that dripped oil. It looked like it had been sucked up in a typhoon, dumped in a swamp and licked by cows before being driven home by way of a ploughed field.

I had got the worst of the mud off with my brush. Underneath the muck, I was quite amazed to find that the van was actually white! I was now beginning the first shampoo. So far, Josh hadn't lifted a finger to help. He wasn't as keen as me. He gets loads of pocket money and new trainers every term. His nan was due for a visit and she always gives him twenty quid. No one had nicked *his* skateboard.

'Don't just sit there,' I said, irritably. 'Come and help me.'

'I am,' said Josh, not moving. 'I'm just having a breather. My back's killing me.'

'Why don't you go and knock on a few doors, then?' I suggested. 'Whip up a bit of custom? If you're not going to help.'

'Whatever,' said Josh, still not stirring from the wall.

'At least get me some more water. There's a tap there, look, you don't even have to go inside.' (It was good when there was a tap in the front garden. It meant we didn't have to trail through people's houses.)

'Actually,' said Josh, 'I think I'll pack it in for a bit. See if my nan's arrived for lunch. We're having chicken.'

'It's all right for some,' I said, coldly. I was standing in a puddle of oily water, soaked through, with numb arms and a blister coming up on my thumb. And now Josh was talking about going off to claim his jackpot twenty quid and get a proper lunch!

No one would be roasting chicken in my house, I knew. It would be full of screaming toddlers in soggy nappies. Some of Kenny's friends were coming round. My mum would be frantic.

'How long are you going to be?' I went on, sternly. 'We've only done four cars. We agreed on ten a day.'

'I know.' Josh gave a shrug. 'But I forgot about my nan coming.'

'Well,' I snapped, 'at least help me finish this one.'

'I can't, man. Mum said one o'clock, and I've got to change. Look, have to go. We'll split the proceeds now. Here's your share.'

He jumped up off the wall, rummaged in his pocket and counted out the money. I got seven pounds.

'It should be nine,' I pointed out. 'Half of eighteen.'

'Ah,' said Josh. 'But you'll be getting four pounds for this one. So I'm taking an extra two. I get eleven now. You get seven and keep the four. So we each end up with the same. That's fair.'

'No, it's not,' I argued. 'If I'm doing the van by myself, I should get the whole amount. And I have to replace the shampoo before my dad finds out. You owe me half for that.'

'Why? I brought the bucket.'

'But the bucket was free. I've got to *buy* the shampoo, haven't I?'

It seemed reasonable to me. Besides, I'd worked hardest. I'd done all the touting for business, and apologising for the bucket. You only had to look at the state of my hands to know I'd done more than my fair share of the actual washing, too. I really needed this money. I was going to fight for it.

Well, not *fight* for it. Not actual fisticuffs. I don't go in for fighting unless I can help it. (Although there was an incident in the playground once, which ended in a trip to the hospital.) No, it wouldn't come to blows. But I wasn't going to take it lying down.

'Look,' said Josh, 'I've done my bit. We agreed

11

to split the profits. I can't help it if my nan's coming, can I? And you don't have to buy more shampoo. You can fill the empty bottle with washing-up liquid. I bet your dad won't notice.'

'As if,' I sniffed, making a mental note because it was a good idea.

'Anyway,' said Josh. 'I haven't got time to talk about it now.'

'What about tomorrow?' I asked, stiffly.

'I can't, man. I've got to go and buy new shoes.'

'Well, thanks for telling me. Thanks a *lot*.'

'I forgot, right? *You* forget stuff sometimes, don't you? Look, I've got to go.'

'So that's it, then?' I said, disgusted. 'You're out of the car-washing business. Yes?'

'Yes,' said Josh, quite stroppy now. 'If you're going to be like that, I am. And if you're that fussed about a lousy couple of quid…' Scornfully, he tossed four pound coins on the pavement. Three fell in the gutter and the fourth rolled under the van. 'There. Take it. See ya.' And he strolled off.

'Great!' I called after him. 'Terrific. Remind me not to pick *you* for a business partner next time.'

'Yeah!' he called, adding, with an airy wave, 'You can keep the bucket.'

'It's a rubbish bucket!' I roared.

'So go stick your rubbish head in it!'

'Yours, you mean!'

And with that, our cutting exchange ended. I had got the last word. Good.

'Tightwad!' shouted Josh, just as he rounded the corner.

So he got the last word. Not so good.

I was hopping mad. I picked up the three coins, crouched down, took a deep breath and rolled under the van.

It was dark and filthy. I peered around and spotted the runaway pound resting in a pool of engine oil. I fished it out, scraped my knuckles putting it into my pocket, rolled over, whacked my head painfully on the exhaust pipe and got an eye full of rust. I lay there, in a puddle, clutching my head and wiping away at my gritty eye. It was then that I saw the feet.

I knew those feet. They were big. The shoes were brown, and had weird buckles. They were topped with thick, lumpy, brown socks that looked home knitted. It was Flora.

Flora lives with her mum in the corner house

of my street. I've known her for ages. She's a bit old-fashioned looking. She's got braces and glasses and wears her hair in plaits. But she draws great cartoons and collects jokes. We kind of like each other. We both think we're quite funny.

'Come out, come out, whoever you are!' sang Flora, underneath the van.

I began wriggling out. In doing so, I accidentally kicked over the bucket that I'd parked by the back wheel. A river of brown suds flowed over my trainers.

Flora was standing on the pavement with a big cardboard box in her arms. She watched me make my sorry entrance, rising from the underworld like the Demon King in a pantomime. I was soaking wet, smeared with oil and had a lump forming on my head. My hair was attractively decorated with leaves, rust, cigarette ends and old chips that someone had dropped in the road.

'Hi, Tim,' she said. 'Why do cowboys die with their boots on?'

'I dunno,' I snapped, picking a chip out of my ear.

'They don't want to stub their toes when they kick the bucket.'

'Huh,' I said, a bit crossly. I wasn't in the mood for jokes, particularly not very good ones. I sat down on the wall and began blotting my sodden feet with an old towel.

'I've got a joke for every occasion,' said Flora, who probably has.

'Shame they're not funny,' I growled, fingering my head lump.

'Oooh! Grumpy! What's that lump on your head?'

'I walked into a revolving door and changed my mind.'

'You've just banged it on the exhaust, haven't you?'

'Yes, if you must know.' Well, I had, and it hurt.

'Have you had a row with Josh Mahoney? I saw him stomping down the street with a face like a squashed slug.'

'Yes, actually,' I said, bitterly. And I told her all about it. I told her about how I'd worked the hardest and done all the talking, while Josh had just stood around. I complained that, unlike Josh, *I* wouldn't be getting any proper lunch, my home having turned into the House of Toddling Demons for the afternoon.

I ranted on about the door-slammers and the old lady with the Peke and Josh taking an unfair amount of money, then making out I was the mean one. She made all the right noises and agreed that right was on my side.

It made me feel better, sounding off to Flora. She knew how much I needed a new skateboard. I'd bumped into her the day after mine had been stolen, when I was in a state of deep depression. She'd cheered me up by telling me a joke about two TV aerials getting married. (The service went on for hours, but the reception was great!)

'...so now I've got to finish this van, then carry on on my own all afternoon,' I finished, finally coming to the end of my tirade.

'Come and have lunch at my house,' offered Flora. 'It'll give you strength.'

I was tempted, but I knew I couldn't afford to slack. If I went back to hers, we'd end up making things, because that's what Flora likes to do. She'd want to make a knight's helmet with a working visor, or a model of the Taj Mahal out of jelly and paper clips. I couldn't afford to get sucked in.

'I'd better not,' I sighed. 'If I sit down I'll never get up again.'

'You can have half of this, if you like,' said Flora, rummaging in her pocket and taking out a slightly fluffy cheese roll. 'I got it at the jumble sale. Only one previous owner.'

She was kidding, of course.

'You've been to a jumble sale?' I asked, interested. I like jumble sales. You can pick up some real bargains. Sometimes I get cheap toys for Kenny. Mum says you don't know where they've been, but once they've been near Kenny, it doesn't matter because they fall apart in five minutes. (Actually, that's not fair. He's quite careful with the ones he likes. Especially his cuddly giraffe, who he calls Jug-Jug, don't ask me why.)

'At the community centre,' explained Flora. 'I got loads of stuff really cheap.'

'Like what?'

'Like a beautiful lemon lampshade for my room. A paintbox, never used. A bottle of scent, still in the wrapping. A useful pad. And some puppets.'

'Puppets?'

'Yep. Wanna see?'

'Go on, then. But I'd better get this van finished.'

Wet jeans flapping around my ankles, I squelched off to fill the leaky bucket from the garden tap while Flora laid out her purchases on the wall.

When I came back, they were all ready for my inspection. I skimmed over the lampshade, which was yellow and, frankly, dull. I approved of the paintbox. I admired the scent, which was a bargain at twenty pence. The pad was useful, I could see that. And then I saw the puppets.

They were lined up in a row – a weird collection of faded old glove puppets, made mostly of scraps of old cloth topped with cracked, papier-mâché heads. Various features were missing – eyes and ears and whatnot. They looked as ancient as the hills – the sort of puppets you might unearth from Methuselah's attic, or pull from a time capsule from the old days. The days when there were hoops and hobbyhorses and a proper nursery to play with them in.

There were six of them: a hideous clown with half his jaw missing; a toothless crocodile that was little more than a green sock with a stitched-on tail; an eyeless policeman with a stuck-on helmet and a tiny truncheon; a sailor with a wooden leg hanging by a piece of thread

18

and a battered princess with a cardboard crown. The princess had really been through the wars. She was missing her entire nose, and her dress was falling apart at the seams. Finally, there was a moth-eaten rabbit. I say it was a rabbit, although it had no ears. It did, however, have a fluffy tail and a felt carrot stuck on one paw, so it seemed a fair assumption.

Flora and I looked down at them. Sadly, they looked up at us. Well, all but the policeman, who had no eyes and couldn't.

'Hmm,' I said, at a loss for words.

'I felt sorry for them,' explained Flora. 'Poor old things. Dumped in a box under a stall. Nobody wanted them. I got the lot for fifty pence.'

'Well, well,' I said, privately thinking that if they were cluttering up *my* space, I'd pay fifty pence for them to be taken away to a landfill.

'You don't like them, do you?' said Flora. She picked up the toothless crocodile, wiggled her hand in and made it prowl along the wall, opening and closing its gummy jaws.

'They look like the cast of *Nightmare On Puppet Street*,' I said. 'They're horror puppets. Cruel parents used to lock naughty children in dark rooms with them in the old days. They'd wake up screaming and beg for them to be taken away.' I put on a silly voice. '*Take them away, Mother! Oh, save us from the horror puppets, do!*'

Grinning, Flora waggled the crocodile in my face.

'He dushn't love ush,' she croaked, in a daft, crocodile voice. 'He dushn't fink we're up to shcratch. He finksh we'll shcare little children. O, deary, deary me, Tim dushn't love ush, I'm gonna weep crocodile tearsh, boo hoo!'

'Get off,' I said, sniggering a bit, pushing the manic lump of bobbing cloth away.

Flora picked up the noseless princess and put her on her other hand.

'What's this I hear?' she squeaked. 'Do I gather the child is less than impressed by our royal presence? And me with a tragic nose infirmity? Off with his head, I say! Sharpen the royal sword, I'll do it now!'

I got sucked in. Daft, I know, but I just couldn't help it. I stuck my poor, raw hand up the policeman and waggled it about.

'Evenin' all,' I croaked, in my best, old-fashioned copper voice. 'What's goin' on 'ere then? Did I 'ear someone makin' idle threats about decapitation? Because I don't take kindly to that sort o' talk on my beat.'

'She did, offisher,' burst in the crocodile, flapping its jaws eagerly. 'But that'sh becaush Tim dushn't love ush. He'sh a puppet hater, he ish. He'sh…'

'Ssshhh!' I said, jumping up and hastily tugging the policeman off my hand.

The door had slammed behind us. The man with the van was coming out to see how I was getting on.

'All right?' said the man with the van. He stared at Flora, who hastily began putting her things back in the box.

'Yep,' I said, dipping my trusty sponge in the water. 'Shouldn't take much longer. Nearly there.'

'You've missed a bit,' said the van man, pointing at a patch of mud on the hubcap.

'I'll get it, don't worry,' I said.

'Well, I'll leave you the cash now. I'm nippin' out. Four, weren't it?'

He handed over a handful of loose change, mostly ten and twenty pence coins.

'Reckon you'll find there's bit more there,' he said.

'Thanks,' I said.

'Nah, you're all right. Doin' a good job. Mind you make sure you turn the tap off properly.'

It wasn't until I'd finished rinsing, wiping, polishing and turning the tap off properly that I counted out the money and found he'd short changed me by fifty two pence.

Honestly. Some people.

Chapter Two

I was nearly dead when I finally got back home. I was so wet that it looked like I'd swum there. My hands looked like wrinkled plums. Alone and unaided, I'd worked my way along my road and done another four whole cars, sustained in my heroic efforts by Flora's cheese roll, which she'd kindly left for me. Despite being my neighbours, nobody had given me any tips, so altogether I had earned the grand total of twenty-eight pounds forty-eight pence. Good, but not good enough.

As I'd expected, the house was in turmoil. Everywhere you went, you tripped over pushchairs, toys, tiny shoes, little puffy jackets, half-eaten biscuits, more toys, carrier bags full of soggy nappies, banana skins, abandoned dummies and orange potties.

Mum was on all fours under the kitchen table with what looked like raspberry jelly in her hair, scraping up some nasty yellowish goo with a knife.

She always dreads Wednesdays. That's when it's her turn to look after Bernard, Rosie and Damian, who are supposed to be Kenny's best friends but really are the demon offspring of three women she knows who've agreed to look after each other's children once a week so they can go shopping, or whatever it is mums do when they're not being mothers.

Bernard, Rosie and Damian. I call them the Three Demons. Kenny doesn't like them much, and nor do I. Bernard shouts, hates fish fingers and won't share. He always takes over the TV remote and screams if you try to take it away. Rosie has watery blue eyes, speaks in grunts, and cries if you offer her a banana. Damian's nose is always running and he only eats spaghetti hoops, which he gets in his hair. His favourite game is sitting in Kenny's yellow tractor and peddling full speed at Alf, our cat, who now spends every Wednesday hiding under the bed in my room.

When I arrived, they were parked in front of the TV in the living room with the door wide open so Mum could see them from the kitchen.

The screen featured a large, blue bear that lives in a house. It was supposed to be Quiet Time, Mum said.

If this was Quiet Time, I'd hate to hear Noisy Time. Demon Bernard was clutching Kenny's giraffe as if it was his own, shouting '*No!*' very loudly if any of the others so much as looked at it. He was sitting on the TV remote. Demon Rosie was standing on Kenny's special cushion, staring at the ceiling and shrieking '*Blah! Blah! Bicky Blah!*' for some mysterious reason known only to herself. Demon Damian was wearing an orange potty on his head and bashing away at our glass coffee table with a plastic hammer.

Poor old Kenny was sitting on his own on the sofa, sucking his thumb and turning the pages of a picture book called *Are You My Duck*? It was clear he'd had quite enough friendship for today, thank you, and just wanted them to leave.

'So how's it going?' I asked Mum, opening the fridge and looking for something – anything – to eat. There was a plate of mashed banana, a kiwi yogurt, a bottle of wine and some cans of beer, which my dad likes. Oh, and some milk and a tub of margarine. That was it.

'What does it look like?' snapped Mum from under the table.

'What time are their mums coming?'

'Soon, thank heavens. What have you been doing? You're soaked!'

'You tend to get a bit wet, washing cars all day,' I pointed out.

'A *bit* wet? You look like you've been dragged out of a pond. What's that lump on your head? What are you doing in the fridge?'

'Looking for food. I'm starving.'

'Well, you'll have to wait. I need to get this kitchen cleared up before you go making more mess. I'll make you something later, when Dad comes home with the shopping. Take those trainers off and change out of those wet jeans. You'll catch your death.'

'Aren't you going to ask me how I got on?' I said, rather hurt. I had asked her about her day. She could have asked me about mine.

'How did you get on? I hope you were careful.'

'Yes, I was. I did nine cars.'

'Nine? That's good.'

'Yeah, but it nearly killed me. I was working on my own all afternoon.'

'On your own? I thought you were with Josh?'

'He went off home and left me to it.'

Mum crawled out from under the table and stood up, looking cross. 'Tim, I thought I said I didn't want you knocking on strangers' doors on your own. I only agreed to this car-washing business if there were two of you.'

'It's not my fault that Josh went off.'

'Maybe not, but you should have come straight home. I thought I could trust you more than that.'

That hurt.

'I only did our road after Josh went,' I said. Well, I had. 'I did the Robinson's Vauxhall and

Miss Price's Mini and Joe Smart's Peugeot and Mr Singh's VW. I didn't knock on strangers' doors.'

Well, I hadn't.

'Even so. You do it with someone else, or you don't do it at all. I asked you what's that lump doing on your head. Have you hurt yourself? Let me look.'

A sudden crash came from the living room, followed by a loud wail. Damian had pulled the lamp flex and brought the whole thing down on top of himself. Rosie and Bernard immediately began to howl in sympathy. Kenny didn't, I noticed. He just sighed, turned a page and carried on looking at ducks.

'There! Now see!' snapped Mum, as if I was to blame, and hurried from the room, my head lump forgotten.

I'm a neglected child.

I pulled off my saturated trainers and trudged upstairs to my room. Alf was under the bed, as I knew he would be. I tried to encourage him out, but he just stared, hollow-eyed, and refused to budge.

I put the trainers on the windowsill to drip dry. I stripped off my wet, filthy clothes, slung them in the basket and found some dry ones. I was pulling on a pair of warm socks, when my mobile rang. It was Flora.

'What's all that screaming in the background?' she enquired.

'Kenny's friends playing.'

'Playing at what? Human sacrifice?'

'I wish,' I said, imagining Damian in a cooking pot with spear-wielding cannibals dancing around. That'd give him something to complain about. He'd be glad if it was just a lamp falling on him then.

'I was thinking,' she went on. 'I could come and help you wash cars tomorrow, if you like.'

'Really?' I said. 'That'd be great. Mum says I can't do it unless there's two of us.'

'Good. See you in the morning, then. Nine o'clock at my place? I've got a better bucket.'

Perfect! The wonky one had finally given up the ghost. I'd chucked it into a skip on the way home. Probably the same one Josh had got it from.

'That's great,' I said again. 'Thanks.'

'No problem. How's your blister?'

'Agony.'

'Know the definition of agony? A man with one arm hanging from a cliff with an itchy bum. See you tomorrow.' And with that, she rang off.

The rest of the evening wasn't so bad, not once the Demons had been picked up and carted off back to the netherworld. Mum restored order in the kitchen and I came down to helpfully pick up things in the living room. I was feeling much better now I had a new business partner. I read *Are You My Duck?* to Kenny, who finally went to sleep upside down on the sofa. Alf came downstairs and tortured his catnip mouse in celebration of Damian's departure.

Dad arrived home in a good mood. His lottery ticket had come up and earned him a tenner. He gave two pounds to me for my skateboard fund, which was nice of him. That meant half a car less. He even offered to deal with the smelly carrier bags full of nappies.

We had shepherd's pie for tea. Mum found some cream to put on my sore hands, some ointment for my head lump and a plaster for my thumb. She dug out some old rubber gloves for me to use the next day. I think she felt a bit guilty for neglecting me earlier.

They let me read at the table as a treat. They could see I needed the rest. I was currently re-reading *Robin Hood*, which is a favourite of mine. We did a play about it at school, where I was a tree, but that's another story.

Before they turned on the television, they had a little chat about Kenny's birthday. Mum said he ought to have a party, because that's what all his playmates did. Bernard had had a bouncy castle at his, she said, and Damian had a grand affair at the community centre, with a real fire engine. Not because the place caught fire, you understand. Because his uncle's a fireman.

Rosie had a dressing-up one, where all the girls came as fairies. I remember Kenny crying before he went, because he didn't like being an elf. He cried when he came home, too, and found that he'd been given a girl's party bag by mistake, making him the proud owner of a pink, fluffy, heart-shaped purse with the words 'Little Princess' written on the front.

'Ridiculous,' said my dad. 'He's three. What's he going to remember?'

'There'll be photos for him to look at, though,' said Mum. 'It's a special occasion, Ray. You're only three once. Besides, I don't want to seem mean. Kenny's always getting invited to parties. He's been to four in the last fortnight. I have to do something.'

'So what are you suggesting? Bouncy castle in the hall cupboard? Fire engine in the spare room?'

'Don't be so silly. I thought just a simple celebration. A nice tea, and balloons, and party bags. A few games. Tim can take the coats upstairs.'

'A noble task, befitting my skills,' I said. 'And one I shall be proud to undertake.' Reading *Robin Hood* always tends to make me break into history speak.

'Just hope you don't have to empty any potties,' said Mum, darkly, and I shut up.

'How many kids?' asked Dad, a bit worried.

'I don't know. A few. Ten, maybe?'

'*Ten?*'

'Something like that. You can organise the games. Pass the Parcel. Hide and Seek. Simple things.'

'No fear,' said Dad, alarmed. 'I've seen what *three* of 'em can do to the house. I don't mind blowing up balloons, but count me out on the games front.'

'What about an entertainer, then?' went on Mum. 'I don't think they cost much. They had a juggling lady at Alex Wilkins' party. I heard she was very reasonable. Quite young. Rather pretty, actually. The children loved her.'

'What does she juggle?' asked Dad, sounding quite interested.

'I don't know. Balls, I suppose. Clubs.'

'Is that all?'

'Well, I don't suppose it'll be knives or flaming torches, will it, Ray? Not at a little boy's birthday party. I'll look in the paper, shall I?'

'Suit yourself,' said Dad. 'But I still think it's a waste of time and money. Wait until he's eight,

33

and I'll take him to a football match. He'll remember that.'

Mum went off to get the paper.

'He won't be eight for another five years,' I pointed out. 'He'll have been to thousands of other kids' parties by then. He might feel resentful.'

'You didn't have a party until you were eight. Did you feel resentful?'

'I don't remember,' I admitted.

'There you are, then!' said Dad, triumphantly.

Mum came back, paper in hand.

'Here we are,' she said. 'I can't find the lady juggler, but how about this? *Mr Happy Chappy The Clown. Magic, Balloons and Games. Shows For All Ages.* Ring him up, Ray, see how much he charges.'

'Why me?' said Dad.

'Why not?' said Mum, and went off to put Kenny to bed.

Chapter Three

'Hello, Tim,' said Flora's mum. 'Long time no see. My, how you're growing!' She stood in the doorway, all pleased to see me. She walks with a stick. Something wrong with her leg, I don't know what.

'Hello, Mrs Ferguson,' I said. 'Is Flora ready?'

'Up in her room. I hear you're off washing cars. What fun! I expect both of you to be multi-millionaires by the end of the day. Treat me to a holiday in the Caribbean.'

'Ha, ha,' I chuckled, politely. 'Let's hope so, yes.'

'Flora says you need a bucket. And I made a few sandwiches in case you get peckish.'

'Great,' I said, brightly. 'Thanks.' I hoped they weren't peanut butter, which I don't like. There's something about the way it sticks to your teeth.

'They're peanut butter,' she said. 'I hope that's all right?'

'Lovely,' I said, not quite so brightly.

'Go on up,' she suggested. 'I'll sort out the bucket.'

So up I went, tapped on the door and said, in my comedy voice:

'Knock, knock!'

'Who's there?' called Flora.

'Dishwasher,' I said.

'Dishwasher who?' asked Flora.

'Dishwashern't de way I shpoke before I had falsh teef,' I replied, hilariously, and went in.

Flora was sitting cross-legged on the floor, with her horrible old jumble-sale puppets surrounding her. She had the princess in her hand, and was sewing up her frock.

I stared around. Flora's room is usually a bit messy, but today it was the worst I'd ever seen it. There were bits of cardboard and scraps of red velvet all over the floor, and pots of paint on every surface. There was spilled glitter. There was a big pair of sharp scissors on the armchair, lying in wait for an unwary bottom. Her bed was piled high with all the stuff she'd had to move out of the way to make space for the tall, imposing construction that stood in the middle of the room.

It was a puppet theatre. Flora had made it out of a big cardboard box. The outside was boldly painted with red-and-gold stripes. A sign shaped like a swirly cloud was stuck on the top, with the words GRAND PUPPET THEATRE painted on in big, swanky letters. There was silver glitter all around the edge, to make it more eyecatching. A long piece of red velvet was stuck to the bottom edge of the box, reaching right down to the floor.

Some shiny gold material had been used to make curtains that hung down on either side of the stage. The back of the box had been painted with a sea scene. In the foreground were cut-out lobster pots, and a propped-up anchor. The background was dark-blue sea, and pale-blue sky. On the far horizon was a pirate ship with a tiny skull and crossbones fluttering from the top mast. Flora's brilliant at art. I was impressed.

'What are you doing?' I asked. A silly question. It was obvious what she was doing. Flora thought it was silly, too. She said:

'Waiting for my prince to come. He's out giving the horse a nosebag. Good thing you caught me before we gallop away.'

'No, I mean, I can see what you're *doing*. But why are you doing it?'

'Why d'you think? For the poor old puppets,' said Flora, breaking off the thread with her teeth. 'They've been rotting in a box for too long. I thought it was time they had somewhere decent to put on a show.'

'I see,' I said, studying the backdrop again. 'I like the backdrop.'

'Thanks. I'm going to do a couple more, so I can change them over.'

I walked around the theatre to see how Flora had made the whole thing so high. What she'd done was balance the box on top of an old wooden clotheshorse, which in turn stood on two piles of telephone directories. The red material fell down in front, blocking off the audience's view of the puppeteers, who would stand in the wide V made by the two arms of the clotheshorse. It was simple, but quite ingenious.

'I haven't written the script yet,' Flora went on, 'but I know the title.'

'What?'

'*Kidnapped at Sea.* A dark tale of heroic deeds and gut-wrenching evil. Want to help write it?'

'Who's going to watch?' I asked.

'I dunno. Who cares? I'm just doing it for fun.'

'Why the sea theme?' I enquired, squeezing onto her cluttered bed. If I were to be co-writer, I needed to know her creative thinking.

'Well, we've got a sailor and a crocodile, so I thought it makes sense.'

'I see,' I said. 'You reason well, fair maiden.'

'I know I do. Are you reading *Robin Hood* again?'

'Verily, that I am.'

'Thought so.'

'No, but what I'm saying is you've got No-Leg the Sailor and No-Teeth the Crocodile. OK, they're watery. But what about Princess No-Nose? And PC No-Eyes? And No-Jaw the Clown? And Little Rabbit No-Ears? How do they fit in?'

'We'll fit 'em in somewhere,' said Flora, confidently, adding, 'And he *has* got a leg. It's wooden, that's all.'

'I'm not even sure crocodiles live in the sea,' I added. 'I think they live in swamps.'

'The one in *Peter Pan* does,' pointed out Flora.

'All right,' I conceded. 'But what about the rest of them?'

'We'll just make up a story to fit the characters. It can start with the servant waking up our heroine, the princess, who is sleeping in her turret room.'

'What servant?'

'Her trusty old butler, who happens to look a bit like an earless rabbit.'

'Fair enough,' I said. Well, it was. I know a teacher who looks like a mole, so why not a butler who looks like an earless rabbit? 'Then what?'

'The sun is shining. She goes outside to play. She has no hint of the nameless terrors that lie in store.'

'The kidnapping, you mean.'

'No, tea with the fairy queen. Of *course* the kidnapping, keep up.'

'OK, OK, just want to get things clear.'

Flora stuck the princess on her hand, waggled it about and said, in her high, princess voice:

'Well, here I am, playing in the woods on this lovely, sunny day. Tra la la la la, I think I'll do a little dance.'

As always, I got sucked in. Car washing forgotten, I started to pull on the jawless clown. I had an idea he might make the perfect evil kidnapper. I was just about to burst into evil kidnapper speech, when a voice came floating up the stairs.

'Shouldn't you two be off? It's twenty-past nine!'

Mrs Ferguson was right. We should be off. Now wasn't the time to be messing around with puppets. We had a business to run.

'So where are we going first?' asked Flora. She was carrying the bucket – a nice red plastic one, considerably better than Josh's.

41

'We'll have to go a few roads away. I've done the close ones. We must away to strange lands, fair lady. Fear not, I will protect you with my sponge.'

'What about Grafton Street?'

Grafton Street was on our way to school. We walked along it every day. Well, most days. Not on holidays or weekends, obviously.

'Who do we know on Grafton Street?' I pondered. That morning, Mum had given me another huge lecture about only going to the houses of people we knew.

'Mr Smallman. We could see if he wants his bike cleaning.'

'Good idea!' I said.

Mr Smallman lives half-way along. He's got a flashy motorbike and a Rottweiler called Duke, who always barks at us through the gate. He's all right, Mr Smallman. He let me try revving his bike when I was six. So is Duke, actually. He just barks a lot, especially if he hasn't seen you in a while. He's got a short memory. But when he remembers he likes you, he gets all friendly and licky. It would be nice to clean Mr Smallman's bike, if he let us. It would make a change from cars.

We walked along the road in silence for a bit. Then, at exactly the same time, we began to speak.

'So No-Jaw the kidnapper leaps out at Princess No-Nose…'

'I can see where PC No-Eyes might fit in, but where does the croc…?'

We both stopped, and burst out laughing. Then we walked on. By the time we reached Grafton Street, we had the basics of a rough plot thrashed out. It was a bit bonkers, I have to say. But it made us both laugh.

Chapter Four

Three cheers for Mr Smallman! He said we could clean his bike! Flora did most of the talking, which made a nice change after Josh's silent ways. I concentrated on making friends with Duke, who did his usual manic guard-dog act when we first arrived, but then decided he remembered us and went all loving.

The bike is kept in the front garden, along with Duke, who guards it. It only took ten minutes to clean, because it wasn't very dirty in the first place. Duke was really excited to have visitors in his garden. He kept pouncing on the sponge in a puppyish way. He knocked the bucket over once, and rolled in the water, then playfully jumped all over us with his muddy paws. But he kept going '*wuff*!' and, on the whole, was quite endearing.

We carried on talking about the puppet show while we worked. We giggled quite a lot. We tried getting Duke to *sit*! And in the end, much to our triumph, he did. He even gave us a paw.

Mr Smallman was really generous. He gave us a fiver and a glass of orange juice each. He was impressed about Duke sitting on command. He said Duke didn't do that for everybody. Then he suggested we try knocking on his neighbour's door. He said she was 'a very nice young lady' and winked. He said we were to tell her Bob recommended us.

Bob. Bob Smallman. Nice name, nice guy.

We said goodbye to Duke, finished the juice and trudged up the next-door lady's path. We didn't strictly know her, of course, but Mr Smallman said she was all right, so she must be.

A smiley lady with messy yellow hair opened the door. I think she'd just got up. She was wearing a pink dressing gown and had a bowl of yogurt in her hand. She said we could do her car, though, when we said Bob had recommended us. She said it was the black BMW parked along the road, and pointed out the tap in the front garden. Then she went in to finish her breakfast.

It was a really nice car – big, black and gleaming, by far the best in the road. There wasn't a mark on it. It was showroom shiny, a glorious vision of silver chrome and polished metal. We peered in through the window. The dashboard looked like something you'd find in a spaceship.

'A three-stroke GI two four,' I said, giving a knowledgeable little whistle. 'What a beauty.' I was hoping to impress Flora with manly, technical words, although I don't have a clue about cars and was just making it up.

'No it isn't,' said Flora. 'It's a Series 5 sports saloon with six-speed manual transmission.'

Oh. She *did* have a clue.

'How d'you know that?' I asked, mortified.

'Read about it in *What Car*?' said Flora. 'I'm a subscriber.'

All this time I've known her and she can still surprise me.

'You have much knowledge of these matters, fair maiden,' I said, feebly. I felt a bit of a twit, pretending I knew about cars.

'Too right I do, goodly knight. I'd stick to skateboards, if I were you. Anyway, it doesn't need washing. It's clean.'

'Still,' I said. 'She wants it doing. Who are we to argue?'

So we got stuck in.

Twenty minutes later, it was all done. It looked exactly the same as when we'd started. Perfectly clean. Not a smear or a blemish on it. We went back and knocked on the door. Out came the smiley lady, wearing clothes and lipstick this time and carrying a handbag.

'All finished,' we chorused, smugly.

'Really? That was quick,' said the smiley lady. 'I'll come and have a look.' And she came down the path, opened the gate, turned right and began walking down the road.

Right? The car was to the left. Flora and I looked at each other, puzzled.

'Um – excuse me?' I called.

'Yes?'

'Where are you going?' I asked, politely.

'To look at my car.'

'But it's not that way,' said Flora.

'Yes, it is.' The smiley lady pointed to a decrepit, rusty heap, parked some way along under a tree that dripped sap and was home to a million pigeons. It was indeed a BMW, but a really, really old one. 'There. See? Oh…'

Her voice trailed off, along with her smile. Even from a distance, you could see the pigeon droppings. It hadn't seen soap since the dark ages.

Flora looked at me. I looked at Flora. Then we both turned around and looked at the smart, new, gleaming vision of beauty back along the road.

We had washed the wrong car!

The lady was very nice about it. She laughed, actually. We offered to do hers, of course, but she said she had to go out, so it would have to be another day. She suggested we try knocking on the door of the owner of the superior black BMW, explain our mistake and hope he would take pity and pay us for our efforts. She said she didn't know him personally, but she thought he lived over the road at number 13. Then she got into her inferior, unwashed wreck and drove away in a cloud of exhaust fumes, still smiling.

'We're not supposed to knock on strangers' doors,' said Flora.

'I know,' I said. 'But four pounds is a lot to lose. And we did a good job. Flash car like that, he's got to be rich. We might get a tip. No harm in trying.'

'All right, then. Let's do it.' And she walked off down the road.

'So who's doing the talking?' I said, catching her up.

'I will, if you like,' said Flora. She could see I was fed up. The car-washing business was taking its toll. This was my second day at it, after all. My hands were wrecked and I was all out of charm.

'Come on. I expect he'll be all right.'

So we walked along to number 13, passing Duke on the way. He started barking ferociously and hurling himself at the gate as though he'd never seen us in his life.

'Calm down, Duke,' ordered Flora. '*Sit*!'

He gave an amazed yelp of recognition. Then, to our great delight, he sat.

We stood on the doorstep of number 13 and rang the bell. After a moment, there came the sound of wheezy coughing and approaching footsteps. The door opened and we found ourselves staring at a small, wiry man in shirtsleeves. He had short, bristly hair with a bald patch on top and fishy blue eyes. His chin was stubbly and there was hair growing out of his ears. A cigarette dangled from his mouth and he had a mug of tea in his hand. He didn't look too friendly.

'Yes?' he wheezed, through a cloud of smoke. 'What?'

'We've come to confess,' said Flora, briskly but pleasantly. She flashed her braces at him in a rueful little smile. 'I'm afraid we've made a mistake.'

'Mistake? What mistake?' The man's fishy eyes narrowed suspiciously.

'I'm afraid we've washed your car by accident.'

Nothing could have prepared us for the reaction. It was as though we'd told him we'd attacked it with sledgehammers, slashed the tyres, then set fire to it and cooked chestnuts in the flames while singing campfire songs.

His jaw dropped open, the cigarette fell from his mouth and his eyes bulged like a frog in shock. The mug in his hand wobbled, spilling tea down his trousers. He didn't speak. Just made a strangled noise, deep in his throat.

'We're terribly sorry,' continued Flora, nervously. 'Um – we normally charge four pounds, but of course, you didn't actually ask to have it done, so we're happy to reduce it to…'

But she didn't have time to finish.

The man smashed the mug down on the hall table and surged forward, elbowing us out of his way. I stumbled over the bucket and Flora bumped into the wall and hit her chin – but if he noticed, he certainly didn't care. He leaped down the steps, raced down the path, burst out through the gate and hared along to where his immaculate car sat in the road, chrome sparkling and bodywork glinting in the sun. Flora and I glanced at each other, and reluctantly followed.

'I don't believe it!' he ground out. He sounded like the man who does that catch phrase on television. 'I simply-do-not *believe* it! Are you *mad*?'

Actually, he said some other words, too, but I've left them out.

'No,' said Flora, rubbing her chin. 'Just mistaken. We thought it belonged to the lady down the road. Sorry.'

'*Sorry*?' spluttered the man. '*Sorry*? Have you any *idea* what you've done?'

He sank into a sudden, gnome-like crouch and laid his cheek on a door panel, squinting sideways at the shiny expanse.

Flora and I stared at each other in alarm. What *had* we done? Apart from wash it?

'What did you use?' he demanded, leaping up again. 'Come on, come on. Don't tell me washing-up liquid! Just don't tell me that!'

Now he was fussily running his nicotine-stained fingers over the bodywork, feeling for invisible bumps or scratches.

'We didn't,' I said. Well, I had to speak up. I couldn't let Flora take all the stick. 'It's proper car shampoo. My dad uses it. Look, here's the bottle.'

He didn't even look. He was walking around now, face a mask of horror, shaking his head and making hissing noises, then dropping down and doing the sideways squint again. You could almost see steam coming from his hairy ears.

'We haven't scratched it or anything,' said Flora. 'We used a soft sponge.' She held out our sponge as evidence. It was looking a bit tired, but you couldn't deny its soft sponginess.

The man stared at it in disgust, then knocked it out of her hand.

'Have you *any idea* about the washing requirements of a car like this?' he bellowed. 'It needs a special cleaner that leaves no residue, you little tosspots! It's got a *special finish*! Use a cheap shampoo on a car like this and you ruin it! *Ruin it*! Out of my way! Let me get to the hose, try and limit the damage! If I can!'

Puce with rage, he bolted into his garden, snatched up a coiled hose that was tucked behind the dustbin and then came racing out, unfurling it behind him.

Three doors up, disturbed by all the commotion, Duke began barking again.

'Stupid!' raged the man, fumbling with the nozzle. 'Stupid, foolish kids!'

'Look,' I said. 'We've said we're sorry. We rinsed it properly. We honestly haven't hurt it…'

'What do you know about it? What do you know about anythin', you mindless little vandals? I've a good mind to call the cops. Where do you live? What are your names?'

Three doors up, Duke stood on his hind legs, barking over the gate like a dog possessed.

'And you can shut up yer racket an' all!' roared the man. Then he turned and pointed the hose right at him!

54

A fierce jet poured out, hitting Duke full in the muzzle. It must have hurt. He gave a surprised yelp, pawed at his eyes and ran away behind the hedge.

Talk about overreaction. Neither of us could believe it. We just stood there like dummies, biting our lips, shuffling our feet and watching him spray water over the bonnet of his precious car. To tell the truth, we were a bit scared. We didn't know what we were supposed to do. Offer to help? Sign a confession? Slink away quietly? Not ask for money, that was certain.

Then he sprayed *us*! He did! He turned round and he pointed the hose at us! Freezing cold water blasted out, soaking us from head to feet in seconds.

That was it. We didn't hang around any longer. Flora picked up the bucket and took off down the street, with me hot on her heels.

'That's right!' bawled the man. 'That's right! You get on out of here, you little devils!'

A short time later, panting and shivering, we sat on a bench at a bus stop to catch our breath. We were shaken, to say the least. It's not often you get screamed at by a stranger, then half drowned in freezing water.

'That was scary,' said Flora, wringing out her cardigan. 'What a horrible man.'

'A nutter,' I agreed, emptying the water from my trainers. 'A complete, out and out nutter.'

'We didn't even hurt his stupid car,' she said.

'You'd think we'd attacked it with a brush made of nail files,' I said.

'Rubbed it down it with a cactus,' said Flora, giggling a bit.

'Washed it with paint stripper,' I said, getting into the swing, adding, 'then polished it with a hedgehog, for that special finish.' (That was inspired.)

Flora rocked with laughter and said:

'Carved our initials with a fork.'

'Set out bowls of cream on top, to encourage all the sharp-clawed stray cats.'

We were feeling a bit better now.

'Then painted it shocking pink,' said Flora after a moment's consideration. 'Or possibly orange.'

'With red spots, like a clown's car,' I added, chortling.

'That's enough of cars now,' said Flora.

'Yes,' I agreed, sobering up. 'It is.'

She reached into her pocket.

'Fancy a sandwich?' she asked. 'It'll settle our nerves.'

She unwrapped the peanut butter sandwiches. I took one, just to be polite. Flora took a huge mouthful of hers. Bird-like, I nibbled at the edge of mine.

'So what do we do now?' she asked, spitting a soggy crumb onto my cheek. 'Sorry.' She can't help it. It's the braces.

''S OK,' I said.

'You don't like peanut butter, do you?'

'Not much.'

'So do we carry on, or what?'

'What do you think?'

'I don't know. You decide. You're the one who needs the money.'

'We *could* carry on,' I said, reluctantly. I looked up at the sky, which had a single, tiny, wispy little white cloud in it. 'We *could*. Although I think it might be about to rain.'

'Or we could go back to mine and dry off. And you could have cheese on toast. And we could practise the puppet show.'

I thought about it. I was soaked to the skin, I still ached all over from the day before and the blister on my thumb had burst. Besides, I'm fond of cheese on toast.

We went back to Flora's and worked on the puppet show. It was a lot more fun than washing cars.

We both agreed we wouldn't mention the incident to our parents. We would have got a lecture for sure, even though it wasn't really our fault. Besides. Washing the wrong car. It made us look silly.

Chapter Five

I gave up on the car washing after that. Well, I had to. Flora was going away to stay with her grandad and I couldn't think of anyone else who would do it with me. Besides, the incident with the horrible hose man had put me off. There might be more child haters out there. I still didn't have enough money for the skateboard, but that's life. I would just have to wait for Christmas.

The rest of the holiday whizzed by. A couple of my mates came back from visiting their relations and I hung about with them. Mum took me shopping for new trainers, because my old ones fell apart with all the water they'd soaked up. The new ones were OK, but not as good as Josh Mahoney's. I saw him in town coming out of the video shop, and I have to admit that his were better. We both pretended not to see each other.

Other stuff happened. My aunty Pamela came to visit, with Dianne, my cousin, and I had to be nice to her. That's difficult, as Dianne's stopped speaking to me since she hit twelve. She's into pop stars and nail varnish and stuff, unlike Flora, who sticks with the jokes.

Dad and I went fishing for a whole day. Well, we spent a whole day driving around the countryside looking for a pond he insisted was there and wasn't. It was a day wasted, actually, although I got quite good at map reading and can now recite the lyrics of Long John Baldry backwards. (Long John Baldry is a long, tall singer my dad likes. He always plays him in the car when Mum's not there. She prefers Celine Dion.)

I finished *Robin Hood* and took it back to the library. I went to the pictures, making a nasty hole in my skateboard fund. The film was *Pirates of the Caribbean 3,* so I talked in seafaring language for days afterwards. And, of course, the dreaded homework had to be fitted in at the last possible moment.

Then it was back to school. I'll gloss over that bit. Nothing had changed, except that Josh and I weren't speaking. But, hey. Who cares?

While I was getting into the swing of school, Mum and Dad were making preparations for Kenny's party, which was the following Saturday. Mum went and bought balloons, squeakers, fancy hats, cardboard plates and enough party food to sink the Titanic. (Celine Dion sings a song in that, about the heart always going on. The *song* goes on, I do know that.)

Dad spoke on the phone to Mr Happy Chappy the clown, to see if he needed anything in the way of props. Mr Happy Chappy said no, he supplied everything himself, although he would need a bit of space to ride his unicycle. Dad said he sounded very professional, if a bit oily. Apparently, he kept calling Dad 'sir' and referring to Kenny as 'our young birthday gentleman'.

I got roped in, of course. I spent a whole evening stuffing rubbish into 15 goody bags. The guest list had swollen by quite a bit, you will notice.

'It's too many,' said Dad. 'We haven't got a big enough table.'

'They're small children, Ray. They can squeeze up,' said Mum, who was looking up cake recipes. Kenny wanted a duck one, but she was too late to order it at the cake shop.

'We'll never fit 16 around this table. What d'you think, Tim?'

'Arrr,' I agreed, in my best West Country accent. 'The varmints'll scuttle the ship. They'll run amok like ship's rats, begorrah.' (Actually, I'm not sure about begorrah. I think that might be another accent.)

'Don't be so silly,' sniffed Mum. 'And stop talking in that stupid pirate voice, I've got enough to think about.'

I don't think any of us were looking forward to the party. Even Kenny. Mum read out the guest list of all the kids she had invited and he didn't look too impressed.

Later, we were sitting on the sofa, reading *Are You My Duck*? for the twenty millionth time. 'Looking forward to your party, Kenny?' I asked.

'No,' he said.

You can't get clearer than that.

'Of course he is,' said Mum, coming in to give him a cuddle. 'You are, aren't you, Kenny? You're going to have a lovely time. Damian's coming, and Ben, and Rosie. There'll be lots of nice things to eat, and a funny clown man, and games and things.'

Kenny said nothing. He'd stated his case, and that was that.

Finally, Saturday arrived. The morning was spent collecting chairs, garden benches and piano stools from kindly neighbours, blowing up balloons, and laying out 16 places on the kitchen table, which we'd made longer by adding the wallpaper table from the cellar. We covered both of them with Spiderman paper tablecloths, so it looked quite jolly.

Mum was busy in the kitchen, chopping carrots like her life depended on it. Dad was lining up mini juice cartons and spreading jam on sandwiches, which he'd cut really small, like we were having the seven dwarfs to tea. Kenny wandered around in his best jumper, clutching Jug-Jug and looking a bit anxious. When I hung up a bunch of balloons, one of them popped and he burst into tears. That's not like him. The tension of this happy day was obviously getting to him.

The guests began arriving at two o'clock, starting with Demon Damian. That was Alf's cue to flee upstairs and hide under my bed. Damian toddled in clutching a wrapped birthday present, which he refused to hand over. When he found he couldn't keep it, he dropped it on the floor and stood on it. Then he went off to look for Kenny's tractor, which Mum had wisely hidden away.

Ben arrived next. He too threw his gift on the floor, then walked up to Kenny and snatched away his giraffe.

Then the rest of them started arriving. Rosie, Gary, Nasim, Chloe, Jasmina, Alex, Ellie – I can't remember all their names. I didn't know many of them. I did know Josh Mahoney's little brother, who's called Adam. Adam's a bit clingy. He was refusing to let his mum put him down. He'd got her in a headlock and wouldn't let go.

'Hello, Tim,' said Mrs Mahoney, fighting to disentangle his frenzied fingers from her hair. 'Haven't seen you for a bit.'

'No,' I mumbled. I didn't like to say that was because I loathed, detested and despised her eldest son. I made an excuse about dealing with coats, and hurried away.

Dealing with coats wasn't so bad, actually. It meant I could stay out of the horrors involved in getting a three year old to hand over a present to another three year old. It was a present, it was wrapped up, as far as they were concerned it should be theirs. Then they had to be peeled off their parents and sat down at the table. Oh, the misery of it. They were squeezed too tight together, and didn't like it. They fell off their chairs. They grabbed at the tablecloth and pulled things over.

Rosie cried because she thought she had to eat a banana. Some kid called Harold had hysterics when his dad tried to tiptoe out. Apparently, he had separation issues. One small girl took one look at the lovely feast, then hurled herself to the floor, where she lay on her back thrashing her legs around, kicking poor little Adam in the stomach with her sparkly pink party shoe. She had eating issues. Ben wouldn't let go of Jug-Jug. Giraffe issues, I suppose.

No sooner had you got one lot seated, another lot would rise and lurch unsteadily away from the kitchen into the living room, like zombies in a horror film.

I just concentrated on the coats. My bedroom was the cloakroom for the day, which is why I was upstairs when the bad thing happened.

I was on my knees trying to get Alf out from under my bed. As usual, he wouldn't come. As I stood up again, something caught my eye out of the window. A car was slowly coming up our road. A big, black, purring, sleek car. It looked horribly familiar. As I watched, it pulled in to the side. Then the driver got out, a scrap of paper in his hand.

Aaargh! It was horrible hose man!

He was peering at the gates, obviously looking for our house number. Help! He had finally found out where I lived and was coming to complain to my parents! He must have found a scratch on the bodywork or something and was about to accuse me!

Heart thumping, I ducked behind the curtain in case he looked up and saw me. This was all we needed, with Kenny's party about to begin. I felt really sick – and not because I'd eaten four sausage rolls, three fairy cakes and half a packet of Jammy Dodgers.

I heard the gate squeak and his footsteps coming up our path. I heard Dad's voice at the door. Then, just as I knew he would, Dad shouted up the stairs:

'Tim! Come down here!'

Down I went, in fear and trembling. Hose man stood at the door. Our eyes met. He looked a bit taken aback when he saw me. His fishy eyes bulged, and a look of loathing crossed his face. Then, to my amazement, his brow miraculously cleared and he bared his yellow teeth in a smile.

'This is Mr Happy Chappy,' said Dad. 'He's got all his gear in his car. Give him a hand bringing it in, would you?'

Whaaaat? Cigarette-smoking, hairy-eared, car-obsessed, water-squirting, dog-bothering, child-hating hose man was Mr Happy Chappy the *clown?*

'I suppose you'll need somewhere to change?' asked Dad, unaware of our mutual recognition.

'Well yes, sir, that would be useful,' said Mr Happy Chappy. 'The bathroom would be fine. If this strong laddie helps bring the stuff, sir, it won't take more than a few minutes.'

He spoke in a very different voice to the one he had used on Flora and me. It was a hearty, jovial, everyone's-favourite-uncle voice. He even patted me on the shoulder. I could hardly believe it was the same man.

'Ray!' came Mum's sharp voice from the kitchen, over a chorus of demonic wailing. 'Get in here *now!*'

'Right,' said Dad. 'Well, I'll leave you to it. I expect you'd like a cup of tea?'

'That'd be very welcome, sir, very welcome indeed,' agreed Mr Happy Chappy, oozing smarmy gratitude as though he'd been offered the elixir of life.

Talk about Jekyll and Hyde. The second Dad turned his back, Mr Happy Chappy morphed back into hose man. His ingratiating smile vanished. He looked down at me, sneered and jerked his head towards the gate, not saying a word.

We walked down the path in silence, taking care not to look at each other. There was bad blood between us. We had a dark history. There was nothing to say.

In silence, we walked down the road to the big, black BMW. In silence, Mr Happy Chappy pressed the remote fob. The lights flashed once, and all the little door locks obediently popped up. In silence, he walked around to the back. In silence, he flipped open the boot.

It was full of clown stuff. Something that looked like an oxygen cylinder, except that it contained that special gas used for blowing up balloons. What's it called again? Helium. There was other stuff, too. A folded unicycle. Juggling clubs. A trombone. A carrier bag full of balloons. A red-and-yellow clown suit in a polythene bag. Two immensely long, bright-blue clown's shoes, with gold stars on. A big cardboard box containing all kinds of bits and pieces – a ginger wig, a daft hat with a flower on, a big, spotty bow tie, a red false nose, a box of greasepaints.

In silence, Mr Happy Chappy reached in, pulled out the helium cylinder and handed it to me. It weighed a ton. Using more force than was strictly necessary, he wedged three juggling clubs under my left armpit and two more under my right. He hung the carrier full of balloons on my wrist. That was it. I couldn't take any more.

Then, still in silence, he hauled out the cardboard box and balanced the long, bright-blue shoes on top. That left the clown suit, the trombone and the unicycle. One of us would have to come back for those.

In silence, Mr Happy Chappy slammed the boot shut and pressed the remote fob, locking it. Gripping the key ring between his teeth, because he didn't have a hand free, he turned on his heel and headed back for our house.

I was just about to follow him when I caught sight of Flora in her front garden. She had her mouth open and was pointing in disbelief at the retreating form of our enemy. I rolled my eyes, shrugged and mouthed '*I know*!' at her.

And then, as if things weren't weird enough already, something else unexpected happened.

Chapter Six

Guess who came trotting around the corner, tail wagging and nose sniffing the air? It was Duke.

Now, Duke's not allowed out unless he's on the end of a lead. Mr Smallman's got a high gate and a thick hedge, so he can't leap over or wriggle through. What was he doing out on his own, all those roads away from home?

He looked like he was enjoying his little outing. He paused to cock his leg against a lamppost, nosed interestedly at half a burger bun lying in the gutter, wisely decided against it and trotted on again. He was the very picture of happiness. Well, he was until he saw Mr Happy Chappy. Then it all changed.

Duke froze to a halt. His ears went flat. Slowly, he sank into a half crouch; back legs tensed and fur bristling. His mouth wrinkled back, showing his teeth.

Mr Happy Chappy had nearly reached

our gate. He turned around to see where I was. And that's when he saw Duke. Mr Happy Chappy turned pale. His mouth fell open with shock. The set of keys dropped from his mouth and fell neatly through the grid of a drain. From where I stood, you couldn't hear the splash, but I'm sure there was one.

Slowly, very slowly, Mr Happy Chappy backed away, edging towards our gate, which was closed.

Duke growled, deep in his chest, doing a really good impression of the Hound of the Baskervilles.

Grrrrrrrrrrrrrrrrrrrrrrrrrrrrrrrrrrrrrrrrrrrrr!

Then he charged! He shot forward like a bullet from a gun and went haring up the road. He went straight past me without a glance, eyes fixed on his enemy, kicking up dust with his paws. It all happened really quickly, like one of those old black-and-white movies, minus the tinkling piano music.

Mr Happy Chappy dropped the box, which fell on its side, spilling its contents all over the pavement. One of the clown shoes fell with it. That left him holding the other. He dropped into a crouch, holding it at arm's length, like a sword. Honestly. The world's most unlikely weapon of defence. A clown shoe. I have to say it looked pretty funny.

Duke carried on running. Mr Happy Chappy raised the ridiculous shoe over his shoulder, all set to whack him one. Then he changed his mind. He said a rather shocking word, which I won't repeat, dropped the shoe, turned, and bolted for his life along the pavement and around the corner. I'll say one thing for him. He had a fair turn of speed.

The shoe bounced once, then rolled into the road, where it was run over by a passing white van. It could have been the one I washed. It was certainly nice and clean.

'Duke!' I roared, with all the authority I could muster. 'Here, boy!'

Flora was shouting his name, too. She came running out from her garden.

At the sound of our voices, Duke did a surprising thing. He slowed down – then stopped. He looked around, a bit confused. Then he looked back up the road. There was no sign of Mr Happy Chappy, dog-hating hose wielder. What there was, though, was a pavement strewn with interesting-looking toys.

Duke began with the red nose. He picked it up with his sharp teeth, crunched, then swallowed. That was for starters. He picked up the bow tie, gave it an experimental chew, then spat it out again. Then he leapt on the ginger wig. He put his front paws on it, lay down, and began tearing at it with his teeth. Great clumps of ginger hair came out, filling his mouth and making him choke a bit.

'Stop it, Duke!' shrieked Flora. I put down the helium cylinder and the clubs, tore the carrier bag off my wrist and began running towards him, with Flora just behind me.

Obediently, Duke stopped eating the wig. He spat out a great gob of ginger hair and shook his head to and fro, coughing a bit and pawing at his muzzle with a front paw. Then his eye fell on the silly hat with the flower on. He pounced on it, picked it up in his jaws and began furiously shaking it from side to side.

That's when I reached him. I snatched at the hat and tried to drag it out from his jaws. Sensing a game, Duke held on.

'Drop it!' I commanded.

'Rrrrrrrrrrrr!' growled Duke, enjoying himself.

I tugged. He tugged harder. The flower fell off and I trod on it with my foot. The hat was covered in slobber and gouged with tooth holes. It was beginning to tear down the middle.

'Duke!' roared Flora. '*Sit*!'

And, incredibly, Duke sat. He tucked his tail in, dropped the ruined hat at our feet and sat, panting, with his big, pink tongue hanging out, obviously hoping one of us would throw it for him.

'Good *boy*!' I said, approvingly.

Flora ruffled his head. Duke rather sweetly offered her his paw.

I started collecting up the spilled items and putting them back in the box. The torn hat. The long, bright-blue shoes, one of which was now in two pieces. The soggy bow tie. The greasepaints, which had fallen out of the tin and lay scattered in the gutter. Not the red nose, obviously. That was gone for ever.

There was still no sign of Mr Happy Chappy.

What I did see, though, was my dad. He came out of the gate holding what looked like a dirty nappy in his hand, clearly on dustbin duty.

'What's going on?' he asked, looking at the three of us in the road. 'Where's the clown?'

'Search me,' I said. 'Went running off. Scared of the dog.'

The dog in question licked my hand, then lay down on the pavement and rolled over, paddling his paws in the air.

'I'll look, shall I?' said Flora. She went to the end of the road and poked her head around the corner. Then she came back again.

'Hiding behind a wheelie bin,' she said.

It was then that we saw Mr Smallman. He came running down the road from the opposite end, holding a lead in his hand. His panic-stricken expression turned to one of huge relief when he saw Duke.

'Thank goodness for that,' he said, striding up and fastening the lead onto Duke's collar. 'Thought I'd lost him. Someone left the gate open, he's been gone for over an hour. Didn't give you any trouble, did he?'

'Not a bit,' said Flora. 'We told him to sit, and he sat.'

'All right, Bob?' asked my dad. 'How's it going?'

'Not so bad, Ray,' said Mr Smallman. 'And you?'

Of course. They knew each other from the days when Dad walked me to school. I'd forgotten that.

'Duke's grown a bit,' remarked Dad, ruffling his fur.

'Yeah,' said Mr Smallman, fondly. 'What you been eating, eh, you daft thing?' he added, picking soggy strands of ginger hair out of Duke's teeth. Duke licked him affectionately on the nose.

'A wig, a hat, and a false red nose,' I volunteered. 'A sort of clown buffet.'

I caught Flora's eye, and we both sniggered.

At this point, we heard a shout. Mr Happy

Chappy came striding back around the corner, his face like thunder.

'You want to keep that dog under control!' he was shouting. 'Flippin' brute went for me! Nearly had me hand off!'

Duke went rigid at the sight of him. He showed the whites of his eyes and growled a bit.

'Easy, boy,' said Mr Smallman, and placed a soothing hand on his head.

'Nearly had me hand off,' said Mr Happy Chappy again. 'Like a bloomin' wild thing. Danger to the public!'

'Really?' said my dad, sounding a bit chilly. 'So that's why you ran off leaving a couple of kids to deal with him, was it?'

'Don't you get shirty with me, pal,' said Mr Happy Chappy. There was no sign of the 'sirs' now, I noticed. 'Look at the damage that's been caused!'

He seized the cardboard box out of my arms, reached in, held up the remains of the ginger wig and shook it under Mr Smallman's nose.

'See this? That's my livelihood, that is. I'll have you up for damages.'

'Don't you threaten me, mate,' said Mr Smallman. 'I could report you to the RSPCA.

I know you've been tormenting my dog. I've seen you.'

'You ain't seen nothing yet, my friend. Look at the state of this hat! See this shoe? And where's my nose?'

'On your face,' said Flora.

That made me laugh. It was all the tension. I didn't mean to, but a little snort got out.

Mr Happy Chappy turned on me.

'Oh, so you think it's funny do you, son? I suppose you think it's funny that my keys are down the drain, too. How'm I supposed to get in the car, eh? My door key was on it as well. How'm I supposed to get in the house? Tell me that. You gonna pay for a locksmith, are you?'

'Hey, hey,' said my dad. 'No need to be like that, friend. It's not his fault.'

'That's right,' agreed Mr Smallman. 'You got a bone to pick, pick it with me, mate.'

Their voices were raised now. Neighbours were looking out of their windows to see what all the fuss was about.

'You go on in, Tim, and take Flora with you,' said Dad. 'We'll sort this out. Go and give your mother a hand. She's waiting to do the cake. It's like a chimp's tea party in there.'

I can't say I was sorry. I hate arguments, especially between grown-up men. The crosser they get, the more they call each other 'mate' and 'pal' and 'friend.' It doesn't make sense.

So we went in. Dad was right. It was chaos.

The table was swimming with spilled drinks and soggy leftovers. The guests had clearly eaten their fill. Damian was pulling Rosie's hair. Adam Mahoney was climbing into the sink. Screams were coming from the living room. Nasim had just bumped his head falling down the stairs, where he wasn't even supposed to be. Poor old Mum was running around trying to deal with it all.

Kenny the birthday boy was the only one still sitting nicely. He was patiently waiting for his duck cake to make an appearance.

Flora found the matches and we lit the candles. Then we all ran around trying to herd everyone back into the kitchen.

'Where's your dad?' asked Mum, when we finally got them rounded up.

'Here,' said Dad, coming in. He looked a bit grim.

'Good. Let's do the cake, then, before they all go mad again.'

So we did the cake. It had come out a bit funny, more like a stork than a duck, but Kenny liked it. He blew out the candles really nicely.

We sang 'Happy Birthday' and he looked a bit shy. Mum took a photograph (which didn't come out, we discovered later). Then she cut up the cake and offered everyone a slice. Nobody wanted any except Kenny. They all wanted to rampage around the house hurting themselves again.

'Is the clown ready?' asked Mum. 'I think we need the entertainment now.'

'Ah,' said Dad. 'Um – there is no clown.'

'What d'you mean, there is no clown? I thought he was in the bathroom, getting ready.'

'Nope,' said Dad. 'He didn't get that far. It's a long story. Just take it from me, Andrea, there is no clown.'

'But how are we going to entertain them?' wailed Mum. 'There's another hour to go!'

Flora and I looked at each other.

'Leave it to us,' we chorused.

Chapter Seven

A record-breaking ten minutes later, we had the puppet theatre all set up in our living room. Mum and Dad kept the toddling hoard in the kitchen while we got prepared. It wasn't easy for them. You could hear the howls a mile away. It sounded like feeding time at the zoo.

'Are you going to be long?' asked Dad, sticking his head around the door. 'It's a mad house in there, your mother's throwing a fit.'

'All ready,' said Flora, calmly. 'You can bring them in now.'

So they brought them in. It took a while and it was a bit of a squeeze, but finally all 16 of them were sitting cross-legged on the floor. Kenny sat right at the front, as he was the birthday boy and entitled to a good view.

I remained out of sight behind the clotheshorse with the earless rabbit on my hand, ready to make its entrance as the faithful old butler. The bedroom backdrop was in place. We were ready.

Flora marched out from behind the theatre and stood in front of the audience, hands on hips.

'This is a show called *Kidnapped at Sea*,' she announced. 'You've got to sit properly and not wriggle. Everybody's got to be really quiet unless we say you can speak. You've got to join in with the songs. And you can boo the baddies. Are we ready?'

'Yes!' chorused 16 little voices.

'Good,' said Flora. 'Then we shall begin.'

And she came to join me. The show was on!

We began with the princess asleep in bed. Flora made her snore really loudly, which brought appreciative giggles from our audience. Then the rabbit butler made his entrance.

'Good morning, Princess Goldipants,' I drooled, jiggling my hand around. 'I am Jeeves, your faithful old butler.'

'Oh, yes, Jeeves, I remember you!' squealed Flora. 'That's because you've lived with me in my lovely castle for the last 17 years.'

'So I have, your highness, so I have,' I intoned, solemnly bowing. 'Did you sleep well?'

85

'Oooh, yes, Jeeves, I did. I had a lovely, lovely dream about a twinkling star.'

'*Did* you, my lady? Fancy that. I do believe I know a song about a twinkling star.'

'Do you, Jeeves? And how does it go?'

'I *think* I remember. But I may need some help from the little boys and girls.' I cleared my throat and burst into song. 'Ahem. *Twinkle, twinkle, little star, how I wonder…*'

The audience obligingly joined in, which was just as well as I'm not a great singer.

After the song, there was more dialogue, which went like this:

Princess   What's for breakfast, Jeeves?

Butler   Smelly-sausage pancakes with stinky-sock sauce.

(*Pause for audience laughter. It took a while coming while they thought about it, but they got there in the end. Kenny thought it was hilarious. I could hear him in fits. He has a very advanced sense of humour.*)

Princess   I think I'll go for a walk in the woods after breakfast. I saw a dear little black sheep there the other day. Do you think he'll be my friend?

Butler   I know a song about a black sheep.

Princess   *Do* you, Jeeves? How does it go?

Butler   Oh, *you* know that one.

Princess   I'm not sure I do.

Butler   Of course you do.

Princess   I really don't think I *do*. Remind me how it goes. I so enjoy your lovely singing voice.

Butler (*firmly*)   No, I really think you do. Start off, and the boys and girls will help you.

(*A hearty rendition of 'Baa Baa Black Sheep', this time led by Flora. Well, I wasn't going to do all the singing.*)

Do you notice how we'd customised the play to fit the age of the audience? We'd simplified it, cutting out all the advanced stuff they wouldn't get. Adding nursery rhymes to pad it out was a stroke of genius, we felt.

At the end of 'Baa Baa Black Sheep', Princess Goldipants and Jeeves said goodbye to each other, and that was the first sensational scene done and dusted.

Flora drew the tiny curtains together. They opened and closed when she pulled a string. It was really clever. Then she quickly changed the backdrop, and we were ready for scene two, in the woods.

Princess   Well, here I am in the woods and

it's such a lovely, sunny day. I think I'll do a little dance and sing a little song. *Oh, the Grand Old Duke of York, he had ten thousand men...*

And so it went on. Most of them joined in, although some didn't know all the words. What do they teach them in nursery these days?

At the end, a little voice piped up, 'Where the black sheep?' but we ignored that, because we didn't have one. But what we *did* have was No-Jaw the clown kidnapper. This was my big moment. I stuck him up behind the princess, and the scene continued.

Kidnapper Ho ho! I see a beautiful princess! I think I'll kidnap her and take her off to sea! I'll make her write a ransom note, and if her father doesn't pay up I'll throw her to the crocodile, ha ha!

I don't think they got the bit about the ransom note, but they knew they were in the presence of a baddy, because my dad helpfully began to boo. Delightedly, they all joined in.

'Boooooooooo!' they screamed.

I could see Kenny through a chink in the red velvet. His eyes were shiny and he was bouncing up and down, clapping his hands, booing like billyo. That was all right, then. On we went.

Princess   Tra la la, tra la la! Oh! Who are you?

Kidnapper Just a kind man, out for a walk. Would you like to come and see my lovely little puppies? I've got three in a basket, over there, behind that tree. Their names are Plip, Plop and Poopy.

(*Short pause while some of them died of laughter at the thought of a puppy named Poopy. Enough comedy. On with the drama.*)

Princess   My daddy says I mustn't go with strangers.

Kidnapper I've got some sweeties, too. Yum, yum, lovely red ones.

Princess (*to audience*) What do you think, boys and girls? Shall I?

(*Pause for audience participation. We were glad to hear that no one thought this a good idea. Their parents had taught them well.*)

'Nooooooooooooo!' they all shouted.

Kidnapper So you're not going to come quietly?

Princess   No, I am not.

Kidnapper In that case, I'll just have to kidnap you.

(*Clown puppet leaps on princess puppet. There is a scuffle. They sink below the stage. End of scene two.*)

Brilliant though it was, I won't repeat all of it. It would take too long. I'll sum it up for you. There were five more scenes, each liberally sprinkled with songs. The kidnapper takes Goldipants to the docks, where she meets a captain of a pirate ship, played by No-Leg the sailor, who sings 'I Saw Three Ships Come Sailing In'. Goldipants gets taken on board ship, and weeps a lot. Everyone sings 'Poor Jenny Sits

A-Weeping'. They land on an island, and get chased by a crocodile. That bit was popular and involved much screaming and booing.

Then a policeman turns up. For no particular reason, he sings 'Humpty Dumpty'. He has been living on the island since losing his way during a routine trip with the river police. That was a bit complicated and I don't think the audience followed our drift here. But they loved the part when he set upon the baddies with his truncheon.

Finally, all the baddies get arrested and carted off to jail, including the crocodile. Goldipants is reunited with her rabbit butler, and the play ends with a rousing chorus of 'Polly Put The Kettle On', because they're going to sit down and have a lovely cup of tea.

And that was it. The end. It took us over half an hour.

Our arms were breaking from holding up the puppets for so long. All the blood had drained out of our fingers. Our throats were sore with singing. It takes it out of you, does puppetry.

But I have to say the show went down well. No, it really did. The kids loved it. They gave us a big clap, and Dad made a little speech about how kind it was of Tim and Flora to put on such a lovely show. Most of them got bored during this and started staggering to their feet and wandering off. Several of them came poking around the back of the puppet theatre. Within two minutes, the curtains had been yanked off the rod and one of the backdrops trampled underfoot. Then Damian gave the clotheshorse a push, and the whole thing went toppling over.

Flora said she didn't care, it had served its purpose. I noticed she didn't let them mess around with the puppets, though. She put them on a high shelf, ready to take home. I think she had become really fond of them. Funnily enough, so had I.

Mum then herded the guests back into the kitchen and gave out the party bags. Everyone got a plastic farm animal, a balloon, a squeaker, wax crayons and a slice of birthday duck. Thankfully, the parents were beginning to arrive to take their little darlings home.

Rather to my surprise, Josh Mahoney came to pick up Adam. He hovered in the doorway with his hands in his pockets. We looked at each other uncertainly.

'Hi,' he said.

'Hi,' I said.

Adam came running up, covered in jam, and trotted on the spot.

'Tim done puppets,' he said. 'I got a squeaker. That girl kicked me. I'm a camel.' (He speaks like this.)

Josh said, 'Go and play, Adam, we're talking, OK?'

Adam galloped off, being a camel.

'So how did it go?' asked Josh. 'In the end? The car-washing business?'

'OK.' There was a pause.

'Did you get a skateboard?'

'Not yet.' There was another pause.

'Look,' he said, 'I'm sorry I forgot about my nan coming.'

'It's OK,' I mumbled, pushing a Twiglet around the kitchen floor with my foot. 'But you didn't exactly *try* did you? I mean, you didn't help drum up any custom. You hardly said a word.'

'I don't like knocking on doors. They're my *neighbours*, man. It was embarrassing.'

He was right. It was. But he wasn't out of the woods yet.

'You didn't do much of the actual work, though, did you?' I persisted. 'You didn't exactly put much effort in.'

'I had a bad back.'

'Oh *yeah.*'

'No, really. I fell off my skateboard the night before. I was in agony.'

'Know the definition of agony?' said Flora, coming up with her armful of puppets. But she saw we were talking, and tactfully withdrew.

'I've been thinking,' said Josh. 'Do you want to buy it? My skateboard?'

'You selling it, then?' I asked. He would be wise to. He's hopeless on a skateboard. Too afraid his trainers'll get mucked up.

'Yep. I'll let you have it cheap.'

'How much?'

'I dunno. Twenty quid OK?'

Twenty quid?!!! That was an incredible bargain!

'OK,' I said. 'You're on.' And we shook hands on it.

'Sorry and all that,' he mumbled. 'About the car-washing business.'

'That's OK,' I said. I picked a plate out of the wreck that was our kitchen table. 'Fancy a sausage roll?'

We were mates again. That was better than OK. It was brilliant.

Chapter Eight

'So did you like your birthday party, Kenny?' I asked.

It was nearly his bedtime, and he was yawning loudly. Mum and Dad were in the kitchen drinking beer, surrounded by a million bin liners. Kenny and I were sitting on the sofa, reading *Are You My Duck?* for a change.

'Mmm,' said Kenny, which could have meant anything.

'What did you like best? The presents? Got some lovely ones, didn't you?'

Kenny looked at his pile of presents, which were displayed on the coffee table. He had cars, a book about tractors, a book about animals, a spinning top, a set of plastic skittles, more cars, a big red ball, a dumper truck, a trumpet and a thing that blew giant bubbles. He was wearing his present from Mum and Dad. A pair of duck-feet slippers and a Spiderman suit.

'Mmm.'

'Or did you like blowing out the candles best?'

He thought about this.

'Puppets,' he said.

Result! I couldn't wait to tell Flora.

I reached behind the sofa, where I had hidden my present to him. I was saving it for a quiet time. I had put both the water gun and the fireman's helmet in a box and wrapped it up with old Christmas paper.

'Got you something,' I said. 'Look. From Tim.'

His eyes widened. He sat up and tore off the paper. He looked in the box. He took out the helmet and stared at it. I put it on his head and did up the buckle, then lifted him up and showed him his reflection in the mirror.

He loved it, I could tell.

We went back to the box.

He took out the water gun and held it, very gently. He was breathing heavily, and his eyes were shining.

He loved that, too.

I showed him how to fill the gun, using water from a vase of dead flowers in the living room that had miraculously survived the party. I didn't want to disturb Mum and Dad, who were still talking in the kitchen.

I opened the window and let him press the trigger and squirt it into the garden. The squirt went for miles. You could vary the pressure, making it spray gently or come out in a strong, fierce jet. It was a terrific gun. I should know. If anyone knows about water pressure, I do. I've used enough hoses in my time.

'Who do you want to take you to bed?' I asked, after he'd had three big goes and knocked over a plant pot on the windowsill. 'Mum, Dad or Tim?'

'Tim,' he said, sleepily.

So I put him to bed without washing his face or cleaning his teeth. I let him wear his duck feet and his Spiderman outfit. He wanted to wear the helmet, too, so I let him. He snuggled down, Jug-Jug in one hand and water gun in the other. It still had a bit of vase water in it and was making his bed wet but, as Mum said, you're only three once.

Then I went down to the kitchen. My parents were on their second beer. Was there no stopping them?

'All done?' asked Dad.

'Yep. He's nearly asleep.'

'I'll pop up and kiss him goodnight,' said Mum, and went out.

Dad reached into his pocket, took out his wallet, extracted four crisp ten pound notes and handed them to me.

'What's this?' I said.

'Money for providing the entertainment,' said Dad. 'Split it between you and Flora.'

'Wow!' I said. 'Really? Wow! Thanks!'

I was in the money! I still had some of the car-washing cash, and I was getting a cheap skateboard. Hey! Things were really looking up.

'You did a good job,' said Dad. 'Nice little show you put on. Made a grown man cry.'

'The kids seemed to enjoy it, anyway,' I said, modestly.

'Yep.'

A little silence fell. Dad took a swig of beer.

'What happened out there in the road?' I asked. 'With you and Mr Smallman and the clown?'

'Oh, we had a little chat,' said Dad. 'I told him I didn't think much of a bloke who'd run off leaving unprotected kids in the road with a Rottweiler. Then blame 'em when he dropped his keys down the drain. He tried to get money out of me, but I told him he could sing for it. Told him he shouldn't go near kids with a temper like that.'

'Wow!' I said. My father the hero. I felt quite ashamed that I'd considered putting washing-up liquid into the empty car shampoo bottle. Tomorrow, I would go out and buy him a brand-new one.

'Flippin' wuss,' said Dad. ''Specially as old Duke's a big softy. You've only got to look at him.'

'I don't think he's too keen on Mr Happy

Chappy, though,' I said, carefully. I didn't want to give too much away. 'I *think* he knows him. I *think* he might live in the same road.'

'So I gather. Bob Smallman's had a lot of trouble with him. Complaining about the barking and whatnot. Last weekend he sprayed the dog in the face with a hose. No wonder it had it in for him. Bob saw the whole thing from the window.'

'Oh.' I had a sudden sinking feeling. 'Did he?'

'Yes. I think you and Flora might have been in the vicinity at the time. Bit of an incident, I hear.'

He was looking at me in a funny way. I said nothing. I just swallowed and blushed a bit.

'I thought we agreed you weren't to knock on strangers' doors?' said Dad.

'I know,' I said, hanging my head.

'Then why did you?'

So I explained. I told him everything about the whole sorry affair. He tried to keep a stern face, but I could see he wanted to laugh.

'Sorry,' I said. 'I won't do it again.'

'Anyway,' said Dad. 'It's all sorted out. Last thing we saw, he was off to ring up a locksmith. That'll cost him a few bob.'

'Will I have to pay for it?' I asked, in a small voice. My dreams of untold riches hung in the balance.

'Course not. Forget about it, it's over. But no more car washing, all right? Go on. Take the money and run. Don't you have homework to do?'

I did, but I wasn't about to do it. I went up to my room and rang Flora.

'Guess what?' I said. 'We've got twenty quid each! For *Kidnapped At Sea*.'

'*Really*?' squealed Flora. She was eating an apple. I imagined bits of it spraying all around.

'Yep,' I said, happily. 'Great, isn't it? That'll pay for Josh's skateboard.'

'You're buying his skateboard?'

'Yep.'

'So you're friends again?'

'Yep.'

'Good,' said Flora. She sounded like she meant it, too.

'I wouldn't choose him for a business partner again, though,' I added.

'A wise decision, good sir knight,' said Flora. 'We make a much better team. Don't you think?'

'I do, fair maiden, verily I do.' I said. 'Arr, avast an' away!' (I was experimentally combining *Robin Hood* and *Pirates of the Caribbean*. I wasn't sure it was working.)

'It was fun, doing the puppet show, wasn't it?' she said. 'I'm quite sorry it's over. I think they liked it, don't you?'

'Kenny certainly did,' I said, and told her about our little conversion.

Flora clucked like a mother hen. 'Small children worship us,' she said. 'Maybe we should start another business. Hire ourselves out as children's entertainers.'

'Hmm,' I said, doubtfully. 'Maybe.'

Then again, maybe not. It had been horribly hot and stuffy in the living room with all those little kids. A bit smelly, too. I wasn't quite sure about spending more time with an audience in nappies. And my puppeteering arms still ached.

'We should think of another fun thing to do,' went on Flora. 'Oh, by the way. I walked by the skip on my way home, and I saw old Happy Chappy's chewed-up wig and daft hat. And the shoes. He must have dumped them in there. Did your dad and Mr Smallman tell him off?'

'They certainly did,' I said. And I told her about that conversion, too.

'…so all in all, I don't think he's a very happy chappy,' I ended.

We both sniggered.

'Seeing his clown stuff gave me an idea,' said Flora. 'We could do a circus. You can be the ringmaster and I'll be the lady on the tightrope. Kenny can be the audience. We could do it next Saturday in my garden. We could ask Mr Smallman if we could borrow Duke. He could be Duke the Wonderdog.'

'Will we have a clown?' I asked.

We both though about this for a moment. Then, together, we said:

'No.'

'Tell you what,' I said. 'We *will* do a circus, but let's leave it for another time. We're in the money, remember? We could go to the fair on the common and splurge. Buy chips, hire a video and go back to yours.'

'Hmm. Will it be *Robin Hood* again? It's just that you've seen it a trillion times.'

'No,' I said, nobly. 'It can be your choice.'

I knew what she'd choose.

'Great! *Bambi* it is, then. And can we make a

Harrier jump jet out of cardboard? I know how.'

'OK,' I said. 'We'll go to the fair, get chips, watch *Bambi* and make a Harrier jump jet.'

And the following Saturday, that's just what we did.

A Word From the Author

A year ago, I wrote a story called *I Am A Tree*, which was inspired by a real-life incident. The main characters were Tim and Flora, and I rather liked them. I filed them away in my head, thinking that I might write another story about them one day.

Nothing happened to inspire me for ages. Then, one morning, two boys on skateboards came to our door and asked if they could wash our car. We said they could, and off they went. When they came back for the money, it turned out that they had washed a neighbour's car by mistake. He wasn't very pleased about it, although I have to say his fury fell far short of that displayed by Mr Happy Chappy.

Round about the same time, I ran across a box full of my old, battered childhood puppets up in the loft. They looked a bit sad. Then, a little boy over the road had a horrifically chaotic birthday party. I met his weary mum, who told me all about it, ending with the words: 'Never again. The next time I'm having an entertainer.'

Washing the wrong car. Skateboards. Old puppets. A toddler's birthday party. Hmm. Slowly, a story began to form in my brain...

Kaye Umansky 2007

I Am a Tree

KAYE UMANSKY

*"They've cast the school play
and I'm a tree!"*

Tim's an ace actor and usually gets the lead
role in the school play, so he's shocked to
find out that this time he's been cast as a tree.
And, what's worse, the only lines he has to
speak are in rhyming couplets! Can anything
be done to help Tim save face, or does this
mean curtains for his acting career?

Black Cats
Books to pounce on

CAPTAIN CODSWALLOP
and the
FLYING KIPPER

MICHAEL COX

*"No Grumpy Roger, no chests of treasure,
no nothing … we're sunk!"*

Captain Codswallop is not having a good day.
While he and his crew have been celebrating
their latest success at sea, a couple of crooks
have stolen their ship. So the pirates set off
to get back the loot. But when a thick fog
comes down and the Spanish Armada turns
up, things start to get complicated…

Black Cats
Books to pounce on

James and the Alien Experiment

Sally Prue

*"The bony hand zoomed right out of the
screen and grabbed him."*

When James is kidnapped by aliens, he
can't believe his luck. They want to
transform his feeble human body and
James can have whatever superpowers he
likes. He chooses super-speed, super-brains
and super-strength. But James soon starts
to realise he might have got slightly
more than he asked for…

Black Cats
Books to pounce on

100% PIG

Tanya Landman

"Oh, Terence. I'm really going to miss you."

Terence the Tamworth boar is proud to
be 100% pig. But his cosy life on the
rare breeds farm is about to change the
day a lorry comes to take him away.
Can Terence escape before it's too late?
And, if he does, how will he cope
with being a pig on the run?

Black Cats
Books to pounce on

Black Cats
Books to pounce on